First published 2000 by Walker Books Ltd
87 Vauxhall Walk, London SE11 5HJ

2 4 6 8 10 9 7 5 3 1

© 2000 Jez Alborough

The illustrations in this book were done in marker pen.

Printed in Italy

British Library Cataloguing in Publication Data
A catalogue record for this book is available
from the British Library.

ISBN 0-7445-7545-1

HUG

Jez Alborough

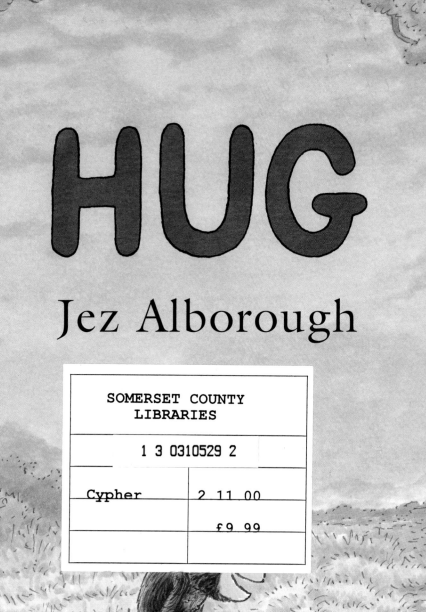

WALKER BOOKS
AND SUBSIDIARIES
LONDON • BOSTON • SYDNEY

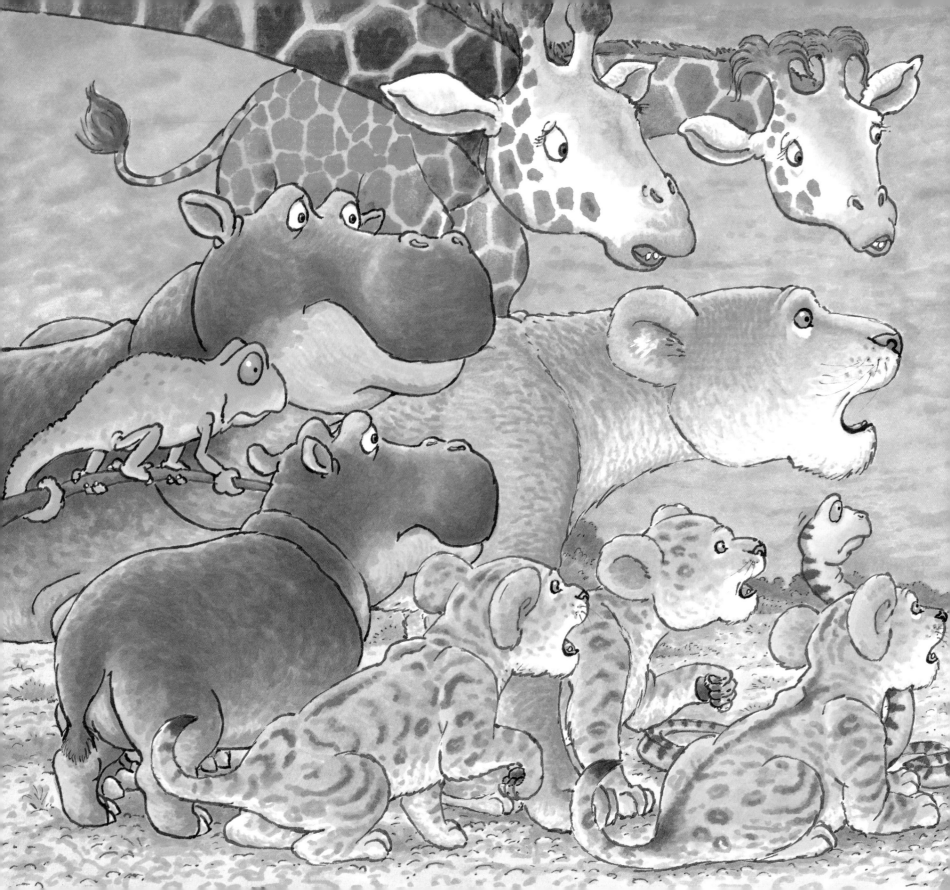

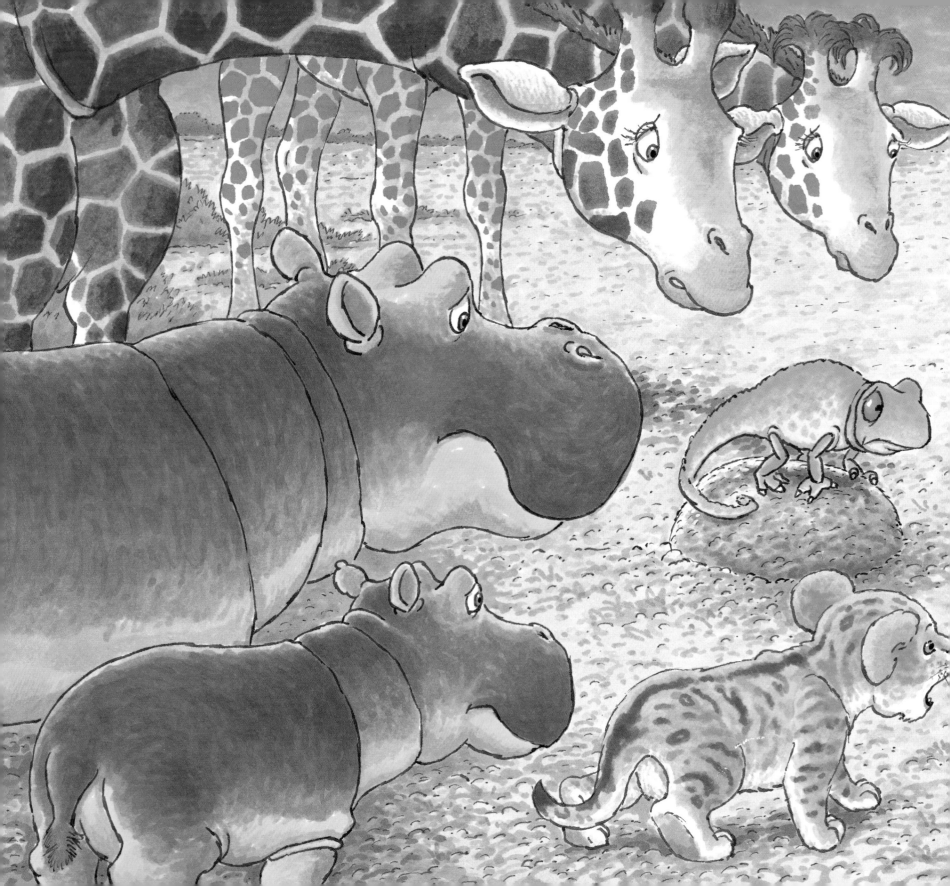

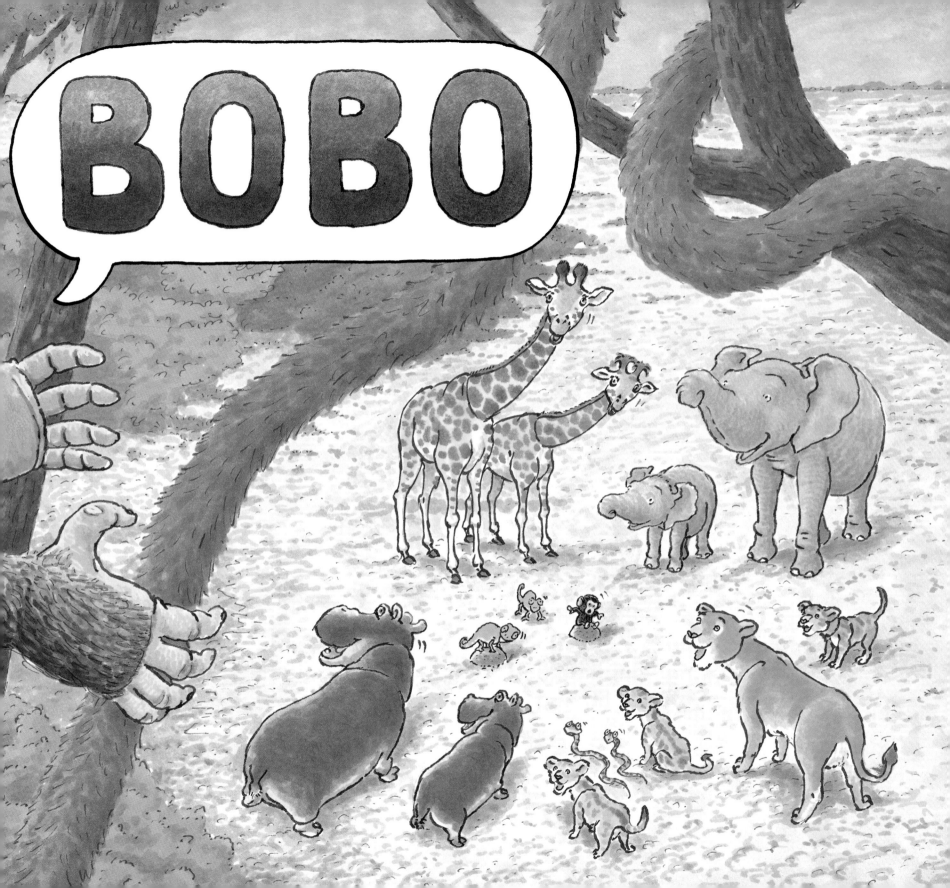